musk ox counts

erin cabatingan

illustrated by matthew myers

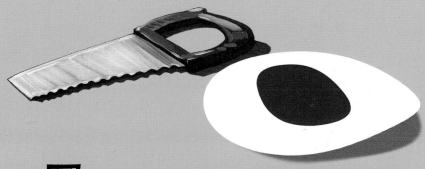

A NEAL PORTER BOOK
ROARING BROOK PRESS
NEW YORK

1 musk ox

Hey!

1 musk ox

What's going on? Where's the musk ox?

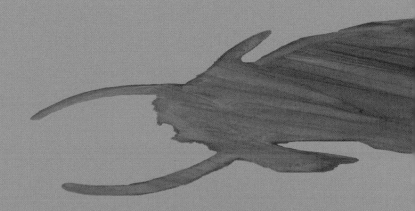

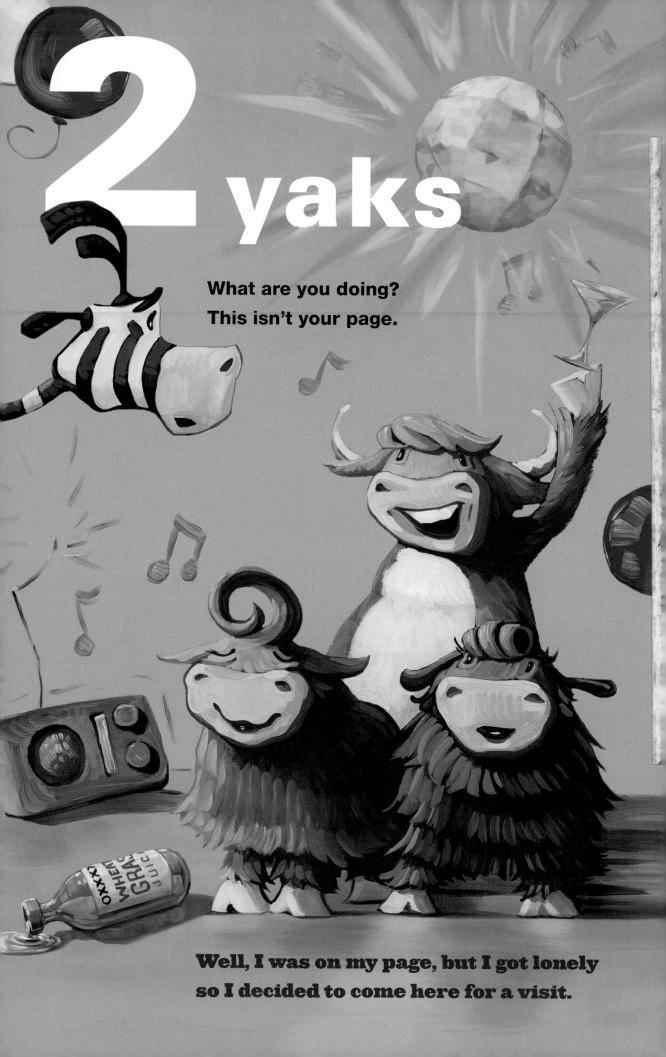

2 yaks

What are you doing?
This isn't your page.

Well, I was on my page, but I got lonely
so I decided to come here for a visit.

But you're ruining the book!
Now there's zero on one
and three on two.

What did you just say?

You need to go back to your page!!

All right, all right.
Keep your stripes on.
I'll fix it. Go and see.

Trust me, it's fixed.

Why would I trust you?

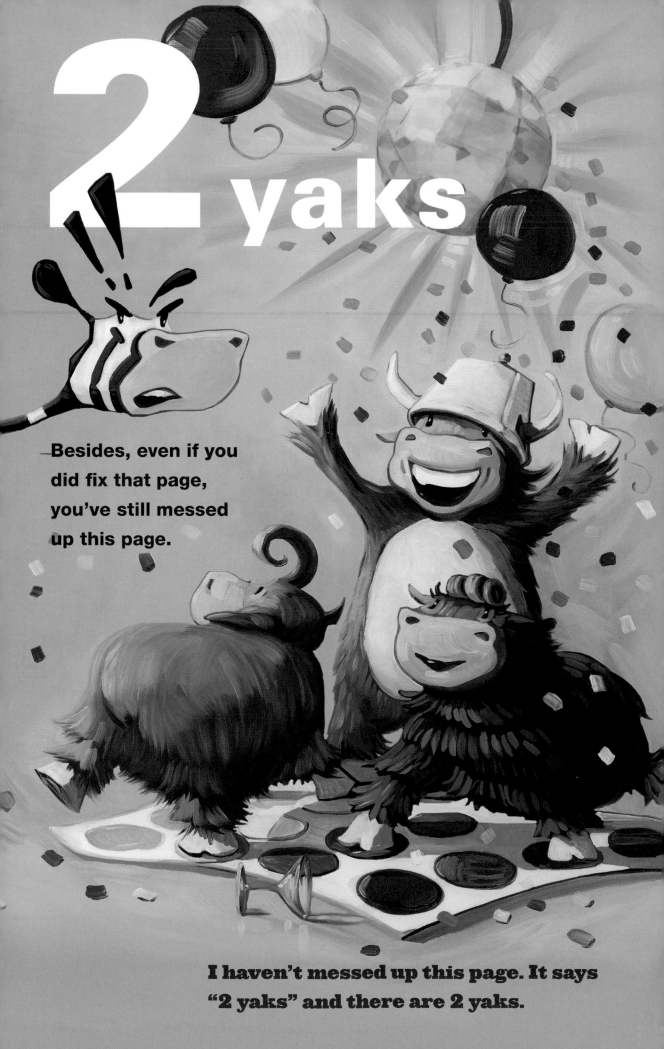

Plus you.
That's 3 animals.

But I'm not
a yak, so
it's okay.

But people might
get confused.

Fine. How about
we make it an
addition book instead
of a counting book?
See, like this:

1 musk ox
+ 2 yaks
——————
= 3 hoofed,
    cold-loving animals

1 musk ox

I've changed my mind. I don't want to be first anymore. It's lonely being number 1.

Don't you dare go
back to number 2.
You've already ruined
enough pages.

Fine. I'll find another one.

3 elephants

Wow. You sure are big. Just like woolly mammoths. I know because musk oxen were alive back in the day.

Would you like to share your page with me? No? Well, the woolly mammoths didn't like us so much either. I'm just going to go find some animals that can't trample me.

4 birds

What are you doing? You just scared the birds away. What are we going to do now?

Don't worry. I've got it covered.

It's a good thing musk oxen have 4 stomachs,* just like cows. Otherwise I don't know what we'd do for this page.

You also have 4 feet.

So? That's not special. Any old ninny can have 4 feet.

I have 4 feet.

My point exactly.

*Technically, it's 4 stomach chambers, but that just sounds weird.

5 goats

Will you please just go back to your own page! Now there are 6 animals on this page instead of 5.

Actually there are 7. You're here messing up the page too, you know.

I'm only here because of you! If you go back to your page, I'll go back to mine, and the book will be just fine.

My page is lonely. But look, this works out great. See, we have ...

$$5 \text{ goats}$$
$$+ 1 \text{ musk ox}$$
$$= 6 \text{ relatives}$$

But what about the 6 snails on the 6 page?

6 snails

I'M WINNING!

Well, even if we don't have
a 6 snails page anymore,
there's still my page.
I'm on 7 zebras.

A page full of zebras?
Let's skip that one.

Why?

So we can be on this page.

$$
\begin{aligned}
& 8\ \text{snakes} \\
+\ & 1\ \text{musk ox} \\
& 1\ \text{whiny zebra} \\
\hline
=\ & 8\ \text{legs}
\end{aligned}
$$

Something about your math is a little confusing.

10 dogs

This is the last page so we'd better be on it. Look, I'll fix it so it says 10 animals and then you take out number 2 over there, and I'll get number 1.

We can't hurt the dogs.

I mean that would be wrong.

Are you calling me wimpy?

BEST IN SHOW

the end

What's wrong?

7 zebras

It's just that I really wanted to have a zebra page and we're at the end of the book.

0 zebras

Text copyright © 2013 by Erin Cabatingan

Illustrations copyright © 2013 by Matthew Myers

A Neal Porter Book

Published by Roaring Brook Press

Roaring Brook Press is a division of Holtzbrinck Publishing Holdings Limited Partnership

175 Fifth Avenue, New York, New York 10010

mackids.com

Library of Congress Cataloging-in-Publication Data

Cabatingan, Erin.

 Musk ox counts / Erin Cabatingan ; illustrated by Matthew Myers,

creators of A is for musk ox. — First edition.

   pages cm

 "A Neal Porter Book."

 Summary: "In this second installment, Musk Ox and Zebra try to make it

through a counting book"— Provided by publisher.

 ISBN 978-1-59643-798-2 (hardcover : alk. paper)

[1. Muskox—Fiction. 2. Zebras—Fiction. 3. Counting—Fiction. 4.

Humorous stories.] I. Myers, Matthew, 1960- illustrator. II. Title.

 PZ7.C1073Mus 2013

 [E]—dc23

                              2012046936

Roaring Brook Press books may
be purchased for business or
promotional use. For
information on bulk purchases please
contact: Macmillan Corporate and
Premium Sales Department
at (800) 221-7945 x5442 or by
email at specialmarkets@macmillan.com.

First edition 2013

Printed in China by Toppan Leefung Printing Ltd., Dongguan City,
Guangdong Province

10 9 8 7 6 5 4 3 2 1